Mongredien, Sue

Clown calamity
/ Sue
Mongredien /
              JS

1686631

For Rachel and Joshua Thulborn,

with lots of love.

S.M.

For Mum and Dad.

T.M.

ORCHARD BOOKS
96 Leonard Street, London EC2A 4XD
Orchard Books Australia
Level 17/207 Kent Street, Sydney, NSW 2000
ISBN 1 84362 566 0 (hardback)
ISBN 1 84362 574 1 (paperback)
First published in Great Britain in 2005
First paperback publication in 2006
Text © Sue Mongredien 2005
Illustrations © Teresa Murfin 2005
The rights of Sue Mongredien to be identified as the author
and of Teresa Murfin to be identified as the illustrator of this work
have been asserted by them in accordance with the
Copyright, Designs and Patents Act, 1988.
A CIP catalogue record for this book is available
from the British Library.
1 3 5 7 9 10 8 6 4 2 (hardback)
1 3 5 7 9 10 8 6 4 2 (paperback)
Printed in Great Britain
www.wattspublishing.co.uk

CLOWN CALAMITY

SUE MONGREDIEN • TERESA MURFIN

ORCHARD BOOKS

Milo Morris liked a laugh as much as
anybody else. He chuckled at comics. He
chortled at cartoons...

He could giggle and guffaw. He could roll
about and roar.

4

Milo's fondness for fun wasn't all that surprising. His parents liked a laugh, too. They were popular party entertainers. Mr and Mrs Morris – or rather, Boom-Boom and Googles – were *fiendishly* funny. They were booked up way in advance.

Boom-Boom – Milo's dad – had a wonky, one-wheeled bike that he rode around on, while he played the trumpet.

Googles – Milo's mum – wore flowers in her hair that squirted water. She could juggle ten balls at once.

They told jokes and sang silly songs and did magic tricks. And every time, their audience would laugh and cheer.

Everyone in Milo's class thought his mum and dad were hilarious. Everyone *except* Milo. He had heard their jokes a billion times. In fact, it was impossible to have a normal conversation *without* jokes.

"Mum, do you know where my football
boots are?" Milo might ask.

"Ahh! That reminds me!" his mum
would reply. "I say, I say, I say. Who
carries a broom in a football team?"

"I don't know, who *does* carry a broom in a football team?" his dad would ask.

"A sweeper!" his mum would cry.

"Boom-Boom!" his dad would chuckle.

"Never mind," Milo would mutter. "I'll find them myself."

It wasn't just at home, either. They cracked jokes at the greengrocer's...

They cracked jokes in the park.

They even cracked jokes at Milo's sports day.

It was enough to drive a boy bonkers.

Then, one day, things got worse. At school, Leo Webster's birthday was coming up and Milo heard somebody ask if he was going to have Boom-Boom and Googles at his party.

"No way!" Leo Webster sneered. "Clowns are for little kids. Clowns are old news."

Leo Webster was the toughest kid in school, so when he announced that clowns were old news, everyone agreed with him.

Milo gulped. Suddenly he had the most un-cool parents in the whole school. This was not good.

Later that day, Milo's parents picked him up from school...in full clown costume.
They had just come from a party. Milo's heart sank when he saw that they'd brought the clown car, as well. Talk about *embarrassing*!

"Hey, kids, does anyone know which part of a car causes the most accidents?" Boom-Boom boomed.

Milo's cheeks burned as he heard the other children sniggering. "Dad – let's go," he said.

"I don't know, which part of a car causes the most accidents, Boom-Boom?" trilled Googles, balancing the car keys on the end of her nose.

"The nut that holds the steering wheel!" guffawed Boom-Boom. "*Boom-Boom!*"

There was a stony silence. Milo jumped into the back seat as quickly as possible. This was awful! *He* had become the class joke – and it was no laughing matter.

Milo's class might have decided that clowns were not cool, but the rest of the town still loved them. With Christmas coming up, Boom-Boom and Googles were so busy they decided not to bother changing out of their costumes between parties. They went to the supermarket in them...

And the post office...

And even the dentist's...

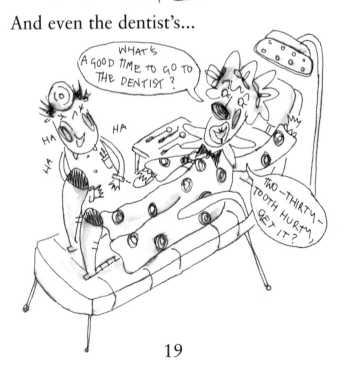

19

Milo never thought he would be pleased to go to school, but suddenly it seemed like the best place in the world. At least while he was there he could escape his embarrassing parents for a few hours.

But one morning, Mr Boffinbrain, the headteacher, had news. "We're having a Christmas party at the end of term," he beamed. "And we've invited Boom-Boom and Googles to entertain us!"

The youngest children all clapped and cheered. But some of the people in Milo's class groaned out loud.

Milo stared at the headteacher, hoping that it was all a wind-up. Or some kind of bad dream, at the very least.

But Mr Boffinbrain, looking very pleased with himself, had already moved onto his favourite subject of playground litter.

He *wasn't* joking, Milo realised with a lurch in his stomach. Mum and Dad were going to be clowning at his school Christmas party. How embarrassing was that?

That evening, Milo decided it was time for some straight talking. "Mum, Dad," he began, "please tell Mr Boffinbrain you won't do the school Christmas party. It'll just be—"

"I say, I say, I say," Googles interrupted, juggling the contents of the fruit bowl.

"*Please*," Milo cried. "Just listen!"

"What do *hedgehogs* have for tea?"
Boom-Boom put in, squeaking his red nose
with a grin. "Prickled onions! Boom-Boom!
Get it, Milo? Prickled—"

But Milo had already left the room.

The last few weeks of school whizzed by.
The infants made paper chains...

And the juniors made mince pies...

Everyone was excited about the
party – apart from Milo. Milo was
dreading it.

On the morning of the party, Milo made one last attempt to tell his parents how he felt. "Mum, Dad," he said earnestly. "*Please* don't show me up today. Everyone in my class thinks clowns are...you know, a bit uncool. And—"

"I say, I say, I say!" his mum exclaimed cheerfully. "What do birds eat for breakfast?"

"I don't know, Googles," Boom-Boom answered, putting on his face paint. "What *do* birds eat for breakfast?"

"I think they're going to give me a hard time about it," Milo said, determined to finish his sentence. "So if you could just—"

"Tweet-a-bix!"

"Boom-Boom!"

What was the point?

The party started after lunch. Mrs Burgess struck up with, "We Wish You A Merry Christmas".

There was Mr Boffinbrain, dressed up as Father Christmas...

There were Miss Kelly and Mrs Turner in elf outfits.

Mr Chinfluff was in a saggy reindeer costume, and Mr Button was wobbling about in a snowman suit.

"Ho, ho, ho!" Mr Boffinbrain called. "I'm proud to present the brilliant, the hilarious, the joke-tastic...Boom-Boom and Googles!"

In cycled Boom-Boom on his one-wheeled bike, tootling his trumpet.

In cartwheeled Googles in her best polka-dot
romper suit and purple wig, squirting water all
over the children in the front row.

Milo looked at the floor. He could hardly
bear to watch.

"Are we meant to be laughing yet?" Leo Webster sneered.

Boom-Boom leaped off his bike and landed with a thud on his enormous comedy shoes. "Hello, kiddiwinks!" he shouted cheerfully. "I'm..." Then he scratched his fuzzy orange wig. "Who am I again?"

"An idiot," said Leo Webster loudly.

"BOOM-BOOM!" shouted the little kids at the front.

Boom-Boom went over to Googles. "Do *you* know who I am?" he asked.

"BOOM-BOOM!" bellowed the little kids.

"You're Googles and I'm..." she started. Then she scratched *her* head. "No, wait a minute. I'm Googles, which means you must be..."

"*BOOM-BOOM!*" screamed the little kids, at the tops of their voices.

Milo had stopped listening. He was
thinking about Christmas Day instead.
Wouldn't it be the most brilliant present if
his mum and dad could, just for one day,
be plain old Mum and Dad again?

Milo sighed as he remembered how Dad used to play football with him before work had taken over.

And Mum had taken him ice-skating, and cycling! They'd spent hours out on their bikes in the good old days.

Milo jumped. His friend Sam was nudging him.

"Ah, there he is!" Googles was saying. "Milo, could you come up on stage and help us, please?"

Milo's eyes boggled in horror. His face turned red as he walked up to the stage.

"We're going to have a little Christmas sing-song now," Boom-Boom told the school. "It's Crasher the Cross-Eyed Reindeer first," he said, plonking a pair of furry antlers on Milo's head. "You can do Crasher's solo."

Mrs Burgess played the opening chords. Milo's mouth fell open. He couldn't quite believe that he was actually there on stage with them. It was like being in the very worst kind of dream. How had he let this happen?

Milo's parents began to sing.

Milo cleared his throat and, with a face as red as Santa's jacket, found himself croaking:

Milo's verse ended, and Boom-Boom started singing again. Milo braced himself to look out at the audience. He could hardly bring himself to see the scornful expressions on their faces...

To his utter amazement, though, most people in the school hall were *smiling* at him, and his parents. They were enjoying it! They were actually enjoying it!

At the end of the song, as Milo went back
to his seat, children he barely knew clapped
him and patted him on the back. It was
a huge relief to sit down again.

"Nice work, Crasher," Sam joked.

Milo rolled his eyes. "Never again," he
said. "You might have enjoyed that – but
I didn't."

"You'd better hope that you get new parents for Christmas," Sam laughed.

Milo pulled off the antlers. "That's not a bad idea," he said thoughtfully.

On Christmas morning, Milo woke up with butterflies. He'd thought very carefully about today. He hoped his idea would work.

After breakfast, Milo and his parents went into the living room to exchange presents.

"These are for you, Dad," Milo said, passing a pile of presents to Boom-Boom. "And Mum, these are yours."

Milo's parents ripped off the paper eagerly.

"My old football boots!" Boom-Boom said, sounding rather confused.

"My ice skates," Googles said, as she opened her first present.

She stroked the leather thoughtfully. "It's been ages since we've been skating, Milo. And what's this – oh, my gardening gloves!" She glanced out of the window with a guilty expression. The garden had become a sprawl of weeds.

"We haven't been out on the bikes for a long time," Boom-Boom said, looking wistful. "Maybe we should all go for a Christmas cycle later?"

"Oh, yes!" Milo burst out. Then he cleared his throat. "Although, I don't think that helmet will fit over your wig."

Milo's mum was nodding. "And we must go skating again together, Milo," she said. "I hadn't realised how much I missed our lessons."

"Me too," said Milo. "But you'll have to take off your comedy shoes to get the skates on, won't you?" His plan was working!

Milo's mum and dad looked at each other. Then they looked at Milo. "I think Milo's trying to tell us something," his dad said.

"I am," Milo said. Then his words came out in a rush. "I'm saying, you're great at being clowns – but sometimes I just want you to be Mum and Dad."

There was a pause. Then Milo's mum removed her wig and Milo's dad pulled off his flashing red nose.

"You're right," his mum said. "Sorry, Milo. The clowns have taken over lately, haven't they?"

"Yes," Milo said. "They have."

After Christmas – and the best family day Milo had had for months – life improved no end. Milo's mum and dad saved their jokes and funny costumes for the parties.

The rest of the time, they were just Mum and Dad. They wore proper clothes again, and had proper conversations, just like any other parents. Best of all, they did lots of things with Milo again.

Milo's dad took him
to play football.

Milo's mum took
him ice-skating.

And they all went
mountain biking in
the countryside,
every Sunday.

58

In fact, thought Milo, as the three of them cycled along, a few weeks later, his mum and dad were quite *normal* these days. It was wonderful! It was...

Boink!

Milo jumped as he was hit on the head by a flying banana.

"Sorry, son," came his dad's sheepish voice. "Just practising a spot of juggling."

"At least it wasn't the pineapple," his mum joked.

Milo found himself laughing. OK, so maybe they weren't *quite* normal. Not totally. But maybe – just maybe – he could live with it.

He cleared his throat. "I say, I say, I say. What happens to bikes when they get old?"

"We don't know. What *does* happen to bikes when they get old?" his mum and dad chorused behind him.

"They get recycled!" Milo laughed. "Get it? They get recycled!"

"Boom-Boom!" they all shouted together, even Milo. "BOOM BOOM!"

FRIGHTFUL FAMILIES

WRITTEN BY SUE MONGREDIEN • ILLUSTRATED BY TERESA MURFIN

Explorer Trauma	1 84362 571 7
Headmaster Disaster	1 84362 572 5
Millionaire Mayhem	1 84362 573 3
Clown Calamity	1 84362 574 1
Popstar Panic	1 84362 575 X
Football-mad Dad	1 84362 576 8
Chef Shocker	1 84362 577 6
Astronerds	1 84362 803 1

All priced at £3.99

Frightful Families are available from all good book shops, or can be ordered
direct from the publisher: Orchard Books, PO BOX 29, Douglas IM99 1BQ
Credit card orders please telephone 01624 836000
or fax 01624 837033 or visit our Internet site: www.wattspub.co.uk
or e-mail: bookshop@enterprise.net for details.

To order please quote title, author and ISBN
and your full name and address.
Cheques and postal orders should be made payable to 'Bookpost plc.'
Postage and packing is FREE within the UK
(overseas customers should add £1.00 per book).
Prices and availability are subject to change.